HEY PRETTY GIRL

JAYDA ARRIVES TO SCHOOL

BY BANECIA BUSH
ILLUSTRATED BY CAMERON WILSON

As Jayda got off the bus at school she had the biggest smile on her face!

Everyone she passed in the hallways stopped and looked at her. Something was different.

As she approached the lunchroom, she was greeted by the school social worker; they call her Mrs. Pam!

"Good Morning Jayda!" Mrs. Pam said; "Good Morning Mrs. Pam. I'll see you at the assembly later, "Jayda replied as she walked down the hall.

"Jayda, you're looking cute today!" said Natalie.

"Thank you girl." Jayda, replied, "Do yall remember when we talked about that commercial they keep showing on t.v. about the girls with clothes on two sizes too small? You know...the one where you could hardly see their eyes? As she laughed.

"Those girls look good, I don't know what you're talking about," said David. "Aint that right Levi?"

Levi uttters, "Riiiiiggghht!"

"Well everybody don't have parents that sit and talk to them like you do Jayda," said David.

"My parents talk to me!" said Natalie. "Mine too!" Kinley replied.

Jackson walked up looked at the class and said, "So...what I learned recently is that you can't be nice to people, I mean...people shady you know...so don't trust these clowns round here."

Next student came up, Nessa...
"Alright Nessa whenever you are ready!" said Ms. Weaver.

Nessa said, "I think that all ya'll just fake to be honest," with so much attitude as she stood there looking at the class with her big green eyes and sassiness.

"That's enough Nessa have a seat," said Mrs. Mckinnie. Nessa folded her arms and walked back to her seat with that same attitude she walked up there with.

"Alright class this project was not a joke, I know those of you that took this as a joke, your grade will reflect the effort you put into this."

"Now, we have two more!" said Ms. Weaver. "Who wants to go first, you Jayda or David?

"Ladies first!" David said with a grin on his face as he looked at Jayda.

"Wow! Is that what you learned?" Jayda asked David.

"Uh nah," I heard a preacher say, "The first shall be last and the last shall be first, I'm about to win this thing! He said with so much pride."

"Bruh you crazy!" Levi said as he laughed.

"Really Levi?" What do you know about a Bruh? Natalie asked.

"Don't worry about what I know worry about picking your face up off the floor when you lose! Levi responded.

"Little boy I'll wipe the floor with you!" Natalie said.

"You tell him Natalie!" Screamed Kinley.

"How bout you wipe the crust off your lips first?" Levi said to Natalie, as he laughed.

"Class, that's enough!" Mrs. Mckinnie said with a serious look on her face. "I'm going to start calling some parents if you don't settle down right now!"

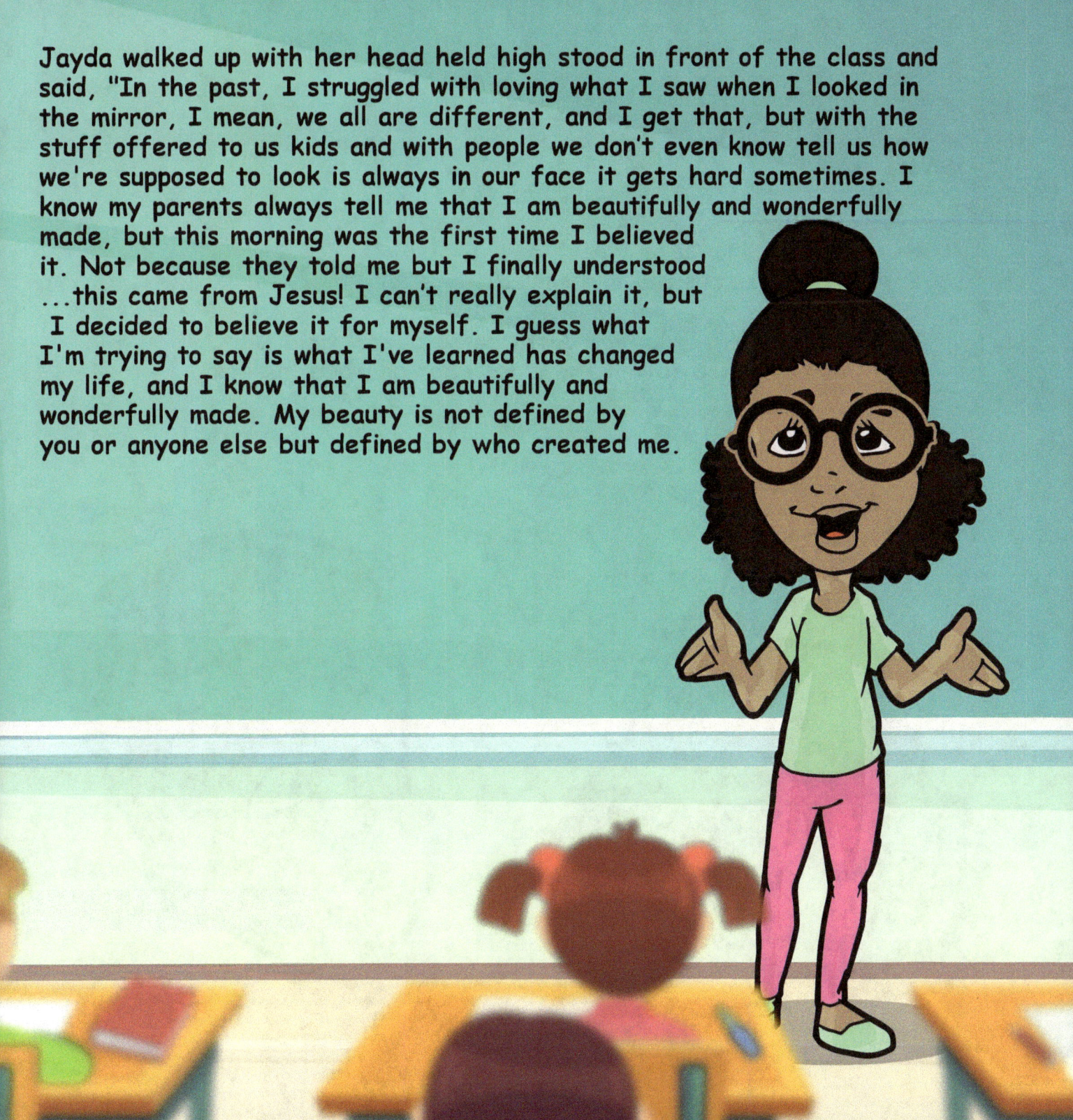

Jayda walked up with her head held high stood in front of the class and said, "In the past, I struggled with loving what I saw when I looked in the mirror, I mean, we all are different, and I get that, but with the stuff offered to us kids and with people we don't even know tell us how we're supposed to look is always in our face it gets hard sometimes. I know my parents always tell me that I am beautifully and wonderfully made, but this morning was the first time I believed it. Not because they told me but I finally understood ...this came from Jesus! I can't really explain it, but I decided to believe it for myself. I guess what I'm trying to say is what I've learned has changed my life, and I know that I am beautifully and wonderfully made. My beauty is not defined by you or anyone else but defined by who created me.

The class clapped and smiled.

"Man Jayda, why you gotta be so deep?" said David as he walked to tell the class what changed his life.

David cleared his throat and said, "My dad told me that I'm a leader, so that means yall supposed to follow me, and that's what I learned, so yall can take it or leave it!"

"Mrs. Mckinnie you have a very interesting bunch," Ms Weaver said as she laughed.

"That I do!" Mrs. Mckinnie responded.
"Alright kids," Ms. Weaver and I are about to decide who wins the Student of Empowerment Award!

"Ok, you all were excited about what you had to say, and in some cases some of you said whatever entered your mind, however, we have a winner," said Ms.Weaver."

Ms. Weaver said, "I have enjoyed my visit in here today" as she laughed. "I learned that I will stick with nursing cause teaching is not for me! So the winner of the Student of Empowerment award is...Jayda!"

HEY PRETTY GIRL
If you're going to trust anybody, let it be the Lord!!
Proverbs 3:5-6

#heyprettygirl
You have what you say!
What are you speaking?
Life or Death?
Proverbs 18:21

#heyprettygirl
Be Thankful! Everybody can't see, hear, walk, talk, etc. Ungratefullness is never cute!
1 Thessalonians 5:18

#heyprettygirl
NEVER let someone with a bad attitude give it to you!!

#HEYPRETTYGIRL
If your heart doesn't match what your lips say, sing, profess it's a lie!

Hey Pretty Girl
FORGET those things
behind you!
MOVE forward!
Philippians 3:13

www.ingramcontent.com/pod-product-compliance
Lightning Source LLC
LaVergne TN
LVHW081546060526
838200LV00048B/2238